Carole C. Bruyère is a writer and an educator with over 25 years of experience in education, dedicating much of her career to shaping young minds and fostering meaningful connections with her students. With undergraduate degrees in psychology and education, Carole possesses a unique blend of academic expertise and personal insight, particularly when it comes to the complex and often painful issue of bullying. Her professional and personal experiences with bullying have given her a profound understanding of its impact and a strong commitment to addressing its effects.

Carole is also a devoted mother of three—Mélanie, Samuel, and Nadine—whose boundless energy and creativity inspire her every day. Fluent in both French and English, she is able to connect with a wide range of readers and audiences, sharing her passion for storytelling and education across cultural divides.

Currently residing in the beautiful Niagara Region of Ontario, Canada, Carole shares her home with her loving husband, John, and their vibrant, diverse family of both human and animal companions. Together, they make for a wonderfully eclectic and lively household.

This book is dedicated to every victim of bullying.
You are not alone!

Carole C. Bruyère

# Welcome to My Life

Victoria's Story

Austin Macauley Publishers

LONDON · CAMBRIDGE · NEW YORK · SHARJAH

**Copyright © Carole C. Bruyère 2025**

All rights reserved. No part of this publication may be reproduced, distributed, or transmitted in any form or by any means, including photocopying, recording, or other electronic or mechanical methods, without the prior written permission of the publisher, except in the case of brief quotations embodied in critical reviews and certain other non-commercial uses permitted by copyright law. For permission requests, write to the publisher.

Any person who commits any unauthorized act in relation to this publication may be liable to criminal prosecution and civil claims for damages.

This is a work of fiction. Names, characters, businesses, places, events, locales, and incidents are either the products of the author's imagination or used in a fictitious manner. Any resemblance to actual persons, living or dead, or actual events is purely coincidental.

**Ordering Information**
Quantity sales: Special discounts are available on quantity purchases by corporations, associations, and others. For details, contact the publisher at the address below.

**Publisher's Cataloging-in-Publication data**
Bruyère, Carole C.
Welcome to My Life

ISBN 9781643789569 (Paperback)
ISBN 9781643789552 (Hardback)
ISBN 9781645365730 (ePub e-book)

Library of Congress Control Number: 2024909503

www.austinmacauley.com/us

First Published 2025
Austin Macauley Publishers LLC
40 Wall Street, 33rd Floor, Suite 3302
New York, NY 10005
USA

mail-usa@austinmacauley.com
+1 (646) 5125767

# Table of Contents

| | |
|---|---|
| Preface | 9 |
| The Big Move | 11 |
| Anxiety | 14 |
| The Neighbors | 17 |
| Back to School | 21 |
| Luke | 32 |
| The Sleepover | 36 |
| Grandma's House | 42 |
| The Presentation | 45 |
| Christmas Break | 49 |
| The Date | 51 |
| Tree | 55 |
| Nicole | 62 |
| Hope | 64 |
| Why Me? | 66 |
| What's Wrong with Me? | 70 |
| A New Day | 75 |

# Preface

I'm telling you my story because even though we might be totally different, we're kind of the same. We both know how much it hurts when friends shut you out and leave you feeling alone. I wish I could make that pain go away for you. But maybe you can turn the hurt into something that makes you stronger.

You know how in movies there's always a hero? Well, I learned I could be my own hero. Yeah, everything completely fell apart for a while, but I had to push through it. When those girls turned on me, and then Luke too… it felt like my heart was breaking. But you know what? Hearts only break when they work in the first place.

I'm super lucky – I know that for sure. I've got my parents and my brother and sister who have my back no matter what.

Their love and support are the reason I can tell you about all this stuff now.

If you don't have a parent you can talk to, find someone else. Maybe a cool teacher, or your grandparents, or that aunt who always gets you, or even a school counselor you trust. Just talk to somebody. It might not fix everything, but having someone really listen helps you feel less alone.

Here's the thing about feelings: they're all over the place! Sometimes you're crazy happy and everything's great, then the next minute you're mad at everyone, or scared about stuff, or jealous –basically, our emotions are like this huge, jumbled mess. But that's just part of being human! When the bad times show up, remember how strong you are. Having all these feelings just means your heart works. There's no shame in that. Life gets super hard sometimes, but you can handle the hard stuff. You can get through this, and you can be your own hero too.

# The Big Move

Moving. Ugh. Wasn't exactly my idea of a summer blockbuster. But my grandpa had a little health scare, and my mom felt terrible about being so far away. So, poof! Our lives were getting packed into boxes.

I wasn't thrilled. My parents tried to sweeten the deal, of course. "Bigger house! Pool! Trampoline!" they'd say. But it wasn't about the stuff. It was about leaving behind everything I knew.

City life was awesome. Street fairs, free concerts, museum exhibits every weekend… it was exciting! We were moving to a place where the highlight of the week was probably bingo night at the community center.

And then there was Tasha – my best friend since forever. We're basically two sides of the same coin. I remember this time in kindergarten when she showed up in a turquoise dress and a tiara. Yeah, we were instant besties. Our sleepovers were epic, even when I used to freak out at bedtime at her house. I knew it was super unlikely, but I was scared that someone might break in and murder me. After a few car break-ins in their neighborhood, Tasha's parents installed security cameras and an alarm system, which cured me of that fear. We had a routine: one weekend at my house, the next at hers – it was the best!

The day of the move was a mix of excitement and sadness. Saying goodbye to our house felt weird, like leaving a piece of my life behind. Sure, our townhouse was tiny, but it was *our* tiny. Turquoise walls, my own bathroom, a basement lair with a giant TV... it was cozy. But we were trading it all for a giant house in the middle of nowhere.

The drive to the new house felt like it lasted forever. Lizzy, my little sister, asked "Are we there yet?" about a million times. My brother Cameron read most of the way. BO-R-I-N-G. We loaded up on Gravol, that motion sickness stuff, because someone usually ended up puking on long trips.

Finally, we arrived. The house was HUGE. Like, mansion-sized. Four parking spots! A wraparound deck! Cameron did a victory lap around the yard.

"Can we pick our rooms?" he asked, his eyes practically popping out of his head.

My mom, to my surprise, said yes! I snagged the biggest room, of course. I am the oldest after all. Lizzy claimed the "princess room" – pink walls, a Cinderella carpet, the works.

I FaceTimed Tasha, giving her the grand tour of my new room. She was so jealous. "Queen-size bed? You're living the dream!" she squealed.

Then why did it feel like a nightmare?

That first night was creepy. An owl was hooting outside, and the house was so empty every unfamiliar sound echoed. It all sent shivers down my spine. I kept checking the alarm system; I must have done it a million times. I tried counting sheep, but my mind was racing. *What if someone breaks in? What if there's a fire? What if that owl smashes into my window?* I finally resorted to earplugs. Eventually, I fell asleep. I guess the melatonin I took before bed kicked in.

Moving is definitely an adventure. Exciting and scary at the same time.

# Anxiety

"I've had a lot of worries in my life, most of which never happened."

– Mark Twain

Waking up the next morning felt like I'd survived the night in a haunted house. But the relief was short-lived. My mind immediately launched into a new round of worries. *What if I failed at school? What if I couldn't make any friends? What if everyone thought I was weird?*

My mom says I've always been like this. As she puts it, "a bit of a nervous Nelly" in new situations. I'd say, I'm a creature of habit. You know, the type who always sits in the same spot on the bus, eats the same cereal every morning and freaks out if their routine gets messed up. Crowds? Forget it. Family gatherings? Let me hide in my room. Please. Change? Not my friend. At first, my parents thought I was just shy, like my dad. Turned out there was more to it.

The fall before we moved, I started getting these crazy stomach aches at night. My parents went full detective, figuring I'd eaten some trigger food. Strawberries were the enemy, then apples, then dairy… it was a food war zone in our house.

But it wasn't food allergies. Dr. Bahr, my doctor, sent me for a million tests – ultrasounds, x-rays, the whole deal. All clear. "Stress," he said.

"Stress? She's eleven!" my dad scoffed.

Mom just nodded.

Then Dr. Bahr had a little chat with my parents behind closed doors. He dropped the "anxiety bomb." Generalized anxiety disorder, to be exact.

Suddenly, everything made sense: Why I couldn't sleep, why I checked the locks ten times a night, why crowds felt like a swarm of bees.

My diagnosis had been like getting a secret decoder ring for my own mind. It had also been kind of scary. Like something was seriously wrong with me.

My mom tried to reassure me. She squeezed my hand and told me about her own anxiety battles. Those deep breaths she was always taking made more sense. She told me that she wished she'd been diagnosed earlier, that it would have helped her understand why she felt so different from everyone else. It was kind of comforting, I guess, but it didn't erase the feeling of being different, of being somehow… broken.

See, with this anxiety thing I have, it's like my brain has a constant low-level hum, always scanning for danger, always expecting the worst. Test anxiety? Check. Social anxiety? Check. Even anxiety about… anxiety! It's non-stop. My body eats all worked up too – sweaty palms, a racing heart, and butterflies in my stomach. Sometimes, it feels like my body is trying to escape from itself.

Dr. Bahr suggested I take a thing called melatonin to help me sleep. After he explained that my worries weren't just butterflies, they were starting to take over my life, I started seeing a therapist. Ruth was amazing, for real. She got me. She taught me breathing exercises that worked like magic. I worried less and even talked to new people. Still terrifying! I was sure I wouldn't find anyone as good as her. But my parents said I had to try. Great. More starting over. More worrying. *What if the new therapist was judgmental? What if they thought I was a waste of time? What if they just didn't get it?*

# The Neighbors

I crawled out of bed and headed to the bathroom, catching the smell of fresh-cut grass. I wondered who opened the window. The bathroom door pushed open, and "Get out!" echoed through the room.

"Lizzy!" I shouted back. "I thought I had the bathroom!"

"Nope," she declared, already brushing her teeth. "New house, new rules."

I rolled my eyes, already dreading the inevitable bathroom battles. I missed having a bathroom all to myself. Sharing with my little sister was going to drive me crazy!

The doorbell chimed a sharp, unwelcome sound that sent a jolt through me. I threw on a hoodie and hoped I didn't look like a total mess. My parents were still asleep, so I tiptoed down the creaky stairs on my way to the door.

A boy, maybe a year or two younger than me, stood on the porch looking like he had a plan. "Hi! I'm Liam. I live two doors down. You have a brother, right?"

He launched into a rapid-fire introduction: "I'm eleven, turning twelve in October. My mom calls me a Halloween monster. I have an older brother, Nick, and a sister, Sophia. How old are you?"

I barely had time to breathe, let alone answer. "Um, hi," I stammered. "I'm Victoria. And yes, I have a brother, Cameron."

Cameron, ever the eager explorer, practically flew down the stairs, his eyes already wide with excitement. "Hi! I'm Cameron! Liam, right?

"Do you want to see my fossils?"

Fossils? My brother, the resident paleontologist. He'd been on a dinosaur kick all summer, devouring books about rocks and minerals. It was a match made in heaven.

As Cameron and Liam disappeared down the street, I couldn't help smiling. *Maybe this move wouldn't be so bad after–!* Another jolt! The doorbell rang again. I opened the door to a girl with a dazzling smile. "Hi, I'm Sophia," she said. "Liam's sister. Want to hang out?"

And just like that, my first day in the new neighborhood took a surprising turn.

Sophia, Liam's sister, was cool. She was older than me, but she wasn't stuck up or anything. We talked for hours about our love for horses, cheesy fantasy books, and the undeniable awesomeness of *Harry Potter*.

"Don't worry about making friends," she said, noticing my nervous fidgeting at the mention of school. "Everyone's in the same boat. I still get butterflies before the first day of school, and I'm already a sophomore!"

I confessed that my mom had given me her usual advice: "Smile and be friendly, and everyone will like you."

Sophia burst out laughing. "Times have changed since your mom was in school," she explained. "The 'popular kids' now are usually the ones who try to make everyone else feel small. Don't let them intimidate you. You'll spot them a mile away."

After lunch, we had a pool party. Liam, Sophia, their brother Nick (who was so cute, though I doubt he even noticed me), Cameron, Lizzy, and me. We played Marco Polo and Colors – my favorite. I always picked turquoise, of course.

Nick was a force in the pool. He was so fast, but incredibly sweet, letting Lizzy win every time they raced.

Cameron and Liam, meanwhile, were deep in conversation about some dinosaur discovery.

The sunset was casting long shadows across the yard. I had the same feeling as before, that this move might not be so bad after all. I had nice neighbors, a cool new friend and the promise of a weekend visit from Tasha.

I thought about what Sophia said earlier about making friends. I'd always been a bit of a people-pleaser, eager to make friends with everyone. But I didn't need to be popular or have the biggest group of friends. I just wanted to hang out with people who liked me for me, people I could trust… like Tasha!

Tasha had always been my rock; we shared secrets and finished each other's sentences. We both had other friends, but our bond was unbreakable. I didn't want friends who smiled to your face but whispered mean things behind your back.

FaceTiming Tasha that night, I poured out all the details – the new house, the pool, the potential new friends.

"You're so lucky!" she exclaimed. "Your own pool! And a yard! I'm so jealous."

"Yeah, but I miss you tons," I confessed, feeling a wave of sadness.

"Don't worry," she said in a warm tone that was totally Tasha. "You'll make new friends. You're amazing, Vic. Everyone will want to be your friend."

Her words were always a total mood booster. Knowing Tasha believed in me gave me the confidence I desperately needed.

That night it was the sound of crickets chirping that replaced the city traffic I was used to. I was still anxious about what was coming. At least I had the rest of the summer to get ready for it. And the rest of the summer was looking pretty awesome.

# Back to School

Ugh, first day of school. "Nooo…" I groaned, pulling the covers over my head and burying my face in the pillow. My alarm clock screamed at me, and I knew I had to get up. My stomach was doing a million somersaults, and I felt like I hadn't slept at all.

My mom was already in the kitchen – looking like a zombie. She's been a teacher for like twenty-five years and still gets nervous about meeting her new students and getting her classroom ready.

"Nervous?" she asked, her voice a little shaky.

"You know it," I mumbled, rubbing the sleep from my eyes. "What if I don't make any friends?"

"Don't be silly," she said, trying to sound cheerful. "You're awesome. Everyone will want to be your friend."

Easier said than done.

Since I was freaking out about missing the bus because I didn't know the stop, my dad drove me to school. As we pulled up, my heart hammered against my ribs. I looked up at the building and saw a giant brick monster. I felt a bead of sweat trickle down my temple. "Deep breaths, Vic," Dad said, squeezing my shoulder. "You've got this."

I tried to take deep breaths, but it was like trying to breathe underwater. Teachers smiled and welcomed us. I still felt like I was drowning.

Kids were everywhere. Some of them were shouting, and others were glued to their phones. Luckily, I found an empty bench where I could slump down. Feeling a wave of loneliness wash over me, I pulled out my phone and texted Tasha: "OMG, I'm here! This place is crazy!"

Scrolling through settings, pretending to text, I tried to ignore the fluttering in my stomach.

A young teacher with a nice smile said, "Welcome to Madison Middle School!" I must have looked totally lost.

"Thanks," I mumbled, trying to smile back.

The next hour was a blur. There was a boring lecture and then we were herded like sheep to our lockers. Everyone was fumbling with their locks, dropping books, and bumping into each other. Finally, I found my locker.

"What school did you come from?" asked Brooklyn, the girl with the locker next to mine.

"I'm new here," I said, feeling a little shy.

"Oh, cool!" she said.

Our homeroom teacher burst into the room like a tornado, yelling, "Alright everyone, gym time!" Brooklyn and her friend Nicole were walking beside me, so I felt some relief. There were crazy games all over the gym. It was like a mini "Amazing Race." Everyone was split into teams of six.

My team? Three boys and two other girls. No Nicole. No Brooklyn. Bummer. There was Ryan, the tallest dude ever, with hair like a bird's nest. He barely smiled and looked super grumpy. Then there was Nadeem, who was flirting with everyone and wouldn't stop talking. He had the longest eyelashes I'd ever seen. I'll admit, I was a little jealous. Next, there was Nathan. He was really small and quiet, but he seemed nice. Aliza. Wow. She was like a tiny superhero. Toned arms, and abs you could see from space. And finally, a girl named Hannah was also on our team. She was wearing SO much makeup it would have given my mom a heart attack!

Our first game was a GIANT puzzle. It was like trying to put together a map of the world blindfolded!

Ryan thought he was the boss. "I'm in charge!" he declared, grabbing the puzzle pieces. Aliza rolled her eyes. "Who died and made you king?" she snapped. Ryan just smirked.

Nadeem stepped in, "Chill out, guys. Let's just work together." He winked at me, and I felt a little flutter in my stomach.

Next up: the obstacle course. It was epic! We had to sprint with a giant ball, crawl through a tunnel that was practically a mouse hole, walk a balance beam without spilling water (super hard!), and jump over and under these crazy barriers.

Aliza flew through the course like a ninja! I'm not the most graceful person, so I felt like a clumsy giraffe trying to fit under those barriers. I kept wondering what everyone was thinking. Were they laughing at me?

Hannah was struggling too, so I cheered her on, "Go, Hannah! You got this!" She smiled at me, and I felt a little better.

Third place after that crazy course. Phew! As we ran to the next game, I noticed a seriously bad smell. BO! *Please don't be me!* I sniffed my armpits. Phew! Just my awesome cucumber deodorant.

The next game was a spaghetti dunk. We had to find flags hidden in a giant pool of spaghetti. Gross! Aliza refused to go in. "No way!" she shrieked. "That's disgusting!"

Nathan, the smallest guy, volunteered. Poor guy! He looked like a walking spaghetti monster when he came out. But he found all the flags!

The last game was a Life Saver pass. We had to pass a Life Saver from mouth to mouth with a toothpick. Sounds easy, right? Wrong! My face was probably the color of a tomato the whole time.

We came in second place! We weren't the winners, but we had so much fun. And I made new friends. So far, a great first day.

Barbecue lunch. I groaned inwardly. Hotdogs and hamburgers? Not exactly my idea of a feast. I'm a vegetarian. But Aliza had invited me to sit with her and her friends. I was so grateful – there was no way I would've asked to join them.

A girl named Lily sat across from me. She was practically a giant compared to me, with dimples that reminded me of a cartoon character. Next to her was Charlotte. Her hair was basically glowing in the sun, and she had an amazing smile.

Remembering what Ruth had told me – people love to talk about themselves – I got brave. "So, what did you guys do this summer?" I asked, trying to sound casual.

And that's all it took. Lily talked about her amazing trip to the beach, Charlotte described her new puppy, and I told them about my summer too.

It felt good. I thought making friends might not be so hard after all.

After lunch, we headed to the sports field to watch the boys play soccer. There was zero shade, but we sat on the sideline anyway.

"So, Victoria," Charlotte grinned, "which one do you think is the cutest?"

I almost choked on my own breath. "Uh…" I stammered, trying to avoid eye contact. "I don't know, they all look pretty good."

"Come on, pick!" Lily teased.

I glanced at the soccer field, trying to play it cool. There was a guy with dreamy blue eyes and a wicked smile. He was definitely a contender.

"Well," I confessed, "I think the one with the blue eyes and light hair in the green shirt is pretty cute."

Lily and Charlotte burst into laughter. "Ooh, you have a type!" Lily teased.

"Maybe," I admitted, feeling my cheeks burn.

At the end of the day, finding my bus was like searching for a needle in a haystack! There were so many of them! When I finally spotted mine, I practically sprinted on and grabbed a seat. No one I knew was there, so I put on my headphones and tried to replay the day in my head. *Did I say something dumb? Was I too loud? Too quiet?* Ugh, I always overthink everything!

Suddenly, the super cute boy from the soccer field was standing beside me. I whipped off my headphones, totally surprised.

"Hey! Can I sit here?" he asked.

"Uh, sure!" I stammered, feeling my face get hot.

"I'm Luke," he said. "You're Victoria, right?"

"Yeah! Hi!" I replied.

"I kind of hoped you'd be in my class," he said smiling at me. My cheeks were burning.

I couldn't stop staring. He had these amazing blue eyes and the cutest dimples. He was a bit shorter than me, which was a little weird, but once he sat down, it wasn't that noticeable. He was very chatty, and I found myself mostly observing him as he spoke. It's a shame he's only on the bus for a few stops.

The walk home from the bus stop felt like I was floating on air. I replayed every detail of my conversation with Luke in my head. *Did I say the right things? Did I laugh at the right times?* I couldn't stop grinning. I was so lost in my own little world that I almost walked right past our house!

Dad was waiting for me on the porch, a huge smile on his face. "How was it?" he asked, giving me a big hug.

"Amazing!" I squeaked, "I met the coolest people and…" I paused, trying to decide whether to tell him about Luke.

"And?" he prodded, raising an eyebrow.

"Well," I said, trying to sound casual, "I met this really nice guy on the bus."

"Oh? What's his name?"

"Luke," I said, feeling my cheeks heat up again. "He was really funny and… and…"

"And?" Dad urged, grinning.

"And he might be kind of cute," I admitted, finally.

Dad laughed. "Well, that's good news! Now, let's hear all about it."

I spent the next hour telling him every detail of my day, from the chaotic cafeteria to the hilarious spaghetti dunk. I even confessed that I might have a tiny crush on Luke.

Mom finally arrived home, looking tired but still beautiful. "Let me shed this armor," she announced, dramatically peeling off her heels. "Then, I'm all yours."

My mom's "teacher mode" includes a strict dress code: skirts, heels, and a whole lot of pearls. Otherwise, after hours, it's comfy pants and t-shirts for Mom!

We all shared stories about our first day. Lizzy, of course, had the most dramatic tales. "Two boys were fighting over who would sit next to me," she declared, puffing out her chest. "It was crazy!"

Cameron couldn't stop talking about the science experiments he was looking forward to. And my mom told us stories about her adorable new class of second graders.

Later that evening we played Monopoly. But the excitement of the first day of school was still buzzing through the house. It wasn't just the start of a new school year; it felt like the beginning of a whole new adventure.

The next morning, I woke up super early! I couldn't wait to see Luke. I was so excited I skipped breakfast. But then, I remembered I had to walk to the bus stop... alone.

Now, this shouldn't have been a big deal, but it was! Anxiety here, remember? Ever since I was little, I'd had this crazy fear of "bad guys." I used to think someone was going to snatch me –any second! It probably started when I was five. Some creep had broken into my mom's car right in our own driveway!

From then on, I was obsessed with locking everything – doors, windows, the whole lot. The thought of "bad guys" getting me was like a scary movie replaying in my head.

As soon as I stepped out the door onto my porch, I started to feel weird. I kept looking back at my house like someone was going to jump out and grab me. When I reached the end of the street, I started to panic. All those years of track practice felt like a waste! I couldn't run if I wanted to. My hands were sweaty, my heart was pounding like a drum, and I felt like I was on fire! I couldn't see my house anymore, and that freaked me out even more. What if someone just pulled over and... you know?

Then, I saw a girl at the bus stop, and I felt a little better. But the real relief hit when I saw the bus! I could finally breathe normally again.

I hadn't even reached school yet, and I was already a mess! All I could think about was seeing Luke. What if he didn't sit with me today? I got so nervous, I casually put my backpack on my lap just in case. When he got on the bus, our eyes met. He grinned and sat down.

"I was hoping you'd take the bus," he beamed. I was too shy to talk, so I just smiled. We didn't say much, but I loved just being near him. We got off the bus together.

"Are you taking the bus home after school?" he asked.
"Yeah!"
"Cool, I'll save you a seat," he said.

I wondered how many times I'd see him that day. I headed to my locker, and there was Brooklyn! She's shorter than me with blonde hair, and she's super pretty.

"Hi!" she said with a huge smile. We walked to class together.

Our teacher, Mrs. Witt, went to high school with my mom. Mom had told her that I get a bit anxious sometimes, and Mrs. Witt kept asking if I was okay. It felt a little awkward. People treat you differently when they know you have anxiety.

Brooklyn and I sat together all day. I found out she had three sisters – two older and one younger. We clicked right away. She's so nice!

For the next few weeks, I mostly hung out with Brooklyn. She was like the Tasha of this school. We texted and Snapped all the time. The only thing I didn't like about her was that she talked about other people behind their backs. It drove me crazy! I wondered if she talked about me too.

It seemed like everyone except me and a few others gossiped. Brooklyn, Nicole, and some of their friends were always making fun of other girls – their hair, their weight, you name it. I didn't get it. Did it make them feel better about themselves? It made me uncomfortable. I tried to ignore them, hoping they'd get the hint.

Soon, Brooklyn and I were calling each other best friends. It was easy to be friends with her. Nicole didn't seem too happy about our friendship though. She gave me the cold shoulder and glared at me sometimes. Brooklyn and Nicole had been best friends since second grade, and they took the bus together. Brooklyn and I weren't trying to show off our friendship, but it was obvious we liked hanging out. We laughed together all the time.

At recess and lunch, most of the seventh graders hung out together. Luke was always there, smiling and flirting with me. I was still shy around him, especially with everyone watching. But we were definitely getting closer. We texted every night. I learned a lot about him. He lived with his mom, his stepdad, and two younger sisters. He never knew his dad. I didn't ask about his dad because I didn't want to pry. Luke was so sweet, always telling me how pretty and amazing I was. Some kids from his old school said he had a bad temper, but I never saw that side of him. He was always so nice to me.

Every night, my mom read most of my texts to make sure they were appropriate. I loved that she cared so much. I told her everything anyway, so I had nothing to hide. Brooklyn said she wished she had a mom like mine.

I know; I'm lucky.

A month into school, Brooklyn and I had our first sleepover! We watched *Twilight* movies and ate junk food in my room. It was so much fun! I finally told her about Luke, and she freaked out!

"What?! Are you serious? Why didn't you tell me?" she screamed.

"I didn't want you to tell everyone at school," I said.

"Oh my gosh, this is amazing! So, is he your boyfriend?"

"Well, not exactly," I said.

"This is so exciting! I'm so jealous. He's so cute!"

"I know, right? You can't tell anyone," I begged.

"I won't, I promise," she said.

I wasn't sure if I believed her, but it didn't really matter. Luke knew I liked him.

On Sunday night, I saw a text from him: 'Hey!'

My mom has always had strict rules about screen time. Weekends are 'free time' – we can watch TV or use our iPads. During the week, we have to do our homework and practice our instruments. Lizzy and I play piano, and Cameron plays guitar. Then, sometimes we play games with Mom, or she lets me text my friends.

I asked if I could text Luke back, and she said yes. He replied right away.

'Hi, beautiful!'

'Hi, how was your day?' I asked.

'Good. I went to my grandparents for dinner,' he said.

'Fun!' I said.

'Are you taking the bus tomorrow?'

'Yes,' I replied.

'Okay, because there's something I need to talk to you about,' he said.

'Oh, should I be worried?' I asked.

'No, no, it's nothing bad,' he said.

'Okay, goodnight. See you tomorrow.'

How was I supposed to sleep?! What was he going to talk about? Was he finally going to ask me to be his girlfriend? He said it was 'nothing bad,' so I had no idea what else it could be! I was so excited I could burst! Then I thought: *Maybe I shouldn't get my hopes up too high. What if he doesn't ask me?*

Ugh, falling asleep was going to be impossible. I vowed to try everything: my melatonin, burying myself in a book and even meditating (which usually just made me think about Luke even more). I decided the sooner I fell asleep, the sooner I'd see him!

# Luke

A million thoughts were racing through my head as I walked to the bus stop. But not one of them was about some creepy guy jumping out of the bushes. Seriously, not ONE. I sat in our usual spot, tapping my foot and practically vibrating with excitement. Luke was going to be on the bus soon!

My stomach was doing a crazy flip-flop thing, my palms were sweaty, and my heart was pounding. Two more stops! Finally, the bus pulled up, and I saw him. My cheeks were probably as red as a stop sign and my forehead was probably shining like a disco ball. I hoped he didn't notice.

He came and sat down beside me, that amazing smile of his, lighting up his whole face. "Hey!" he said.

"Hi!" I squeaked back, feeling all shy and stuff.

We sat there for a minute, and then he said, "So, I was wondering... would you like to be my girlfriend?"

My jaw literally dropped. I was like, "Whoa!" I was super excited, but also kind of freaking out. My mom said no boyfriends, and I didn't want to get in trouble. But there was no way I could say no to him. She'd understand, right?

"Yes," I whispered, feeling a blush creep up my neck. I couldn't believe it! I actually had a boyfriend!

Best. Day. Ever.

He even walked me to my locker! It was so sweet. I didn't tell Brooklyn a thing at school. I wanted to savor the moment. In class, Mrs. Witt gave us a group project on natural disasters. Brooklyn and I were about to pair up when this girl named Lucy asked if she could join us.

"Sure!" we said. Three brains are better than two, right?

Honestly, I'm not a big fan of group projects. I like to know exactly what's going on and make sure everything is perfect, you know? I guess I'm a bit of a control freak, but I really work hard, and I want to make sure everyone pulls their weight.

We decided to do our project on wildfires. Brooklyn took the lead on researching the key factors, such as causes, effects, and where they typically occur. Lucy was researching a recent wildfire in Canada – how it started, the damage, and how much it cost. My job was to figure out how the fire affected the people who lived there, the effects on firefighters, and how to prevent future fires.

Lucy was really cool. She had this awesome style – always wearing pants, usually camo, and never any makeup. Her friends were mostly guys. She had a best friend named Matthew, and they went hunting together with his dad. She said she never really fit in with the other girls. I liked her a lot.

Luke and I saw each other a few times during the day, but I was too shy to talk to him. We talked a bit on the bus ride home, and he said he'd text me later.

I waited for my mom to get home, feeling super nervous. She knew that I liked Luke a LOT, and she'd been a bit strict about boyfriends. I knew she trusted me, but still, I was a little scared.

I worked on my project until I heard the front door open. I tried to stay calm, but I could feel my heart pounding.

"Hi Mom! How was your day?" I asked, trying to sound casual.

"You look different! What's going on?" she asked, looking concerned.

"Nothing much, but I have something to tell you… in private."

"Can I assume this is good news?" she asked, smiling.

"Yes, I think so," I said, grinning.

"Meet me upstairs in three minutes," she said.

I walked into her room, feeling like I was going to vomit. I tried to do those deep breathing exercises Ruth had taught me, but it wasn't really working.

"You can do this," I whispered to myself.

"So, you know Luke, the guy I like?"

"Yes!"

"Well, he asked me to be his girlfriend today."

"Oh my gosh! No way! That's amazing!"

"You're not mad?" I asked, a little worried.

"Why would I be mad?"

"Well, you said I was too young for a boyfriend."

"Listen, sweetie, I'll never be ready for you to grow up. I want to keep you little forever. But I also know what a boyfriend means at your age. I know you'll tell me everything, and I trust you completely."

"So, you're really okay with it?"

"Yes, I'm thrilled for you!"

I hugged her so tight! I was so relieved. I always worry about stuff for no reason.

Luke texted me right away.

"Hi, girlfriend, "he texted.

"Hi, boyfriend. He he."

"Your hair looked really pretty today"

"Aww thanks," I replied. "You looked so cute, as always."

"Thanks!"

He asked me what my friends thought of us. I told him I hadn't told anyone yet, except for a little bit to Brooklyn. I liked to keep my stuff private.

"Oh no, are you mad that I told my friends?" he asked.

"No, not at all! I just figured everyone would find out eventually."

"Oh, okay!"

"Sorry to cut this short, I need to go to bed," I wrote.

"Okay, sweet dreams. I'll definitely be dreaming of you," he texted. Then he sent a bunch of heart emojis and a kissy face.

I sent him a kissy face back and said, "See you tomorrow."

"Looking forward to it," he replied.

I finally drifted off to sleep, still buzzing from the excitement.

# The Sleepover

Saturday, finally. Brooklyn and Lucy had been working their butts off all week, and we were really proud of our presentation. We were planning to meet at Brooklyn's house in the afternoon to put together our display board and practice our speeches.

Then she invited us both to stay over! Sleepovers? Me? Never! Well, except for Tasha's. I started to panic. Maybe I could tell them about my anxiety. *What if they laughed at me? What if they thought I was a total weirdo and didn't want to be friends anymore? What if the whole school found out?* My mind was racing!

I tried to calm myself down. I took a deep breath, held it while I counted to five, then slowly let it out. I did that a few times to chill out. Ruth magic. I missed her. I decided to say yes to sleeping over then fake a stomach-ache later that night. That way, my parents could come pick me up and I wouldn't have to actually spend the night. Genius.

I put on a brave face and tried to act super excited about the sleepover, even though my stomach was doing a million flip-flops.

We met at Brooklyn's house. I brought the display board, markers, stencils, and my laptop. Brooklyn's parents were never home. They were both nurses, so they always worked crazy hours. As soon as I walked in, I noticed their alarm system panel right next to the front door. That made me feel a little better. Maybe a sleepover wasn't such a bad idea.

We gossiped for the first hour about all the boys in our class. Brooklyn and Lucy were on a roll.

"Did you see Britany's bra situation?" Brooklyn whispered, giggling. "They're practically hanging out! So embarrassing!"

"Maybe her mom hasn't bought her a new one yet," I said, starting to feel a little awkward.

"Yeah, right," Brooklyn scoffed. "I bet all the guys are totally checking her out."

"I bet she never showers," Lucy chimed in, making us both burst out laughing.

"And have you seen how much Jessica eats? She's going to explode!" Brooklyn exclaimed.

"She needs to go on a serious diet," Lucy agreed.

I felt guilty. It was like they were judging everyone. I didn't like it. "Guys, maybe we should stop talking about other people like that," I said.

They just shrugged and kept going.

"Okay, okay, let's get this project done!" I said, trying to change the subject.

Lucy was amazing with the art stuff. She decorated the board with these super cool stencils. Brooklyn mostly just played on her phone, but I don't think she was really slacking off. Her part was mostly done.

Two hours later, our board was looking awesome! We just had to practice our speeches. We decided to take a break and have a major junk food fest.

Brooklyn raided the pantry! Bowls were overflowing with chips, chocolate, and candy. I grabbed a plate and piled it high, even though my stomach was already starting to grumble. I have a serious sweet tooth, though, so I couldn't resist.

Then we played "Truth or Dare." Most of the dares were totally disgusting! I had to eat a spoonful of garlic, mustard, and sauerkraut. I almost gagged! Brooklyn had to lick dog food, and Lucy had to drink a mixture of salad dressing and soy sauce. We were laughing so hard we were spitting food everywhere!

For some of the dares, we had to run outside and yell random things like "I love Justin Bieber!" and "I like looking at guys' butts!" It was hilarious!

When it was Brooklyn's turn to answer a truth question, I decided to ask her something that had been bugging me. "Tell me the truth, why doesn't Nicole like me?" I asked.

"She doesn't dislike you," Brooklyn said.

"Well, she's always giving me the cold shoulder and ignoring me," I said.

"She told me that you were 'stealing' me away from her," Brooklyn revealed.

"Nicole's totally crazy like that," Brooklyn explained. "She needs to be in control of everything. If she feels like she's losing a friend, she gets super mean. We used to be best friends, but we fought all the time. One time, she didn't talk to me for a whole month because I liked the same guy she did. It was the worst!"

"Wow, that's intense!" I said. "I don't think I could be friends with someone like that."

We finally got back to our presentation and practiced our speeches. We were a little nervous, but mostly excited to show everyone what we'd done.

Brooklyn's parents had left cash for pizza, so we were in for a feast! While we waited for the pizza to arrive, she suggested we play a prank call game. We dialed random numbers and asked the weirdest questions. Brooklyn went first, putting the phone on speaker so we could all hear.

"Hello?" an old lady's voice squeaked.

"Yes, how can I help you?" Brooklyn asked, trying to sound serious.

"Well, you called me!" the lady snapped.

"No, you called me!" Brooklyn argued.

"I did not! You called me!" The lady sounded furious.

"Don't you think I'd know if I called you?" Brooklyn teased. Lucy was trying so hard not to explode with laughter.

The lady slammed the phone down. We were howling!

"Your turn, Victoria!" Brooklyn said.

"No way! I'm too shy," I whined.

"Come on, it'll be fun!" Lucy insisted.

So, I picked up the phone and dialed a random number. A man answered, 'Hello?'

"Hi, how are you doing? It's been ages!" I said, trying to sound like an adult.

"I'm good,' the man replied. 'Who is this?"

"It's me! Don't you recognize my voice?" I asked, offended.

"Sounds familiar, but I can't place it," he said.

"What?! You don't know who I am?!" I yelled, then hung up. We were rolling on the floor laughing.

It was getting late, and I started to worry. *Could I actually spend the night? I didn't want to ask if they used the alarm; I was afraid they'd think I was a baby. Should I just go home? What if they thought I wasn't having fun?*

Ugh, I always overthink things! I texted my mom. She always knows what to do.

"Hi Momma," I texted.

"Hi, sweet pea! Having fun?" she replied.

"'Yep!" I texted back.

"Good! Need me to come get you?" Even though I hadn't told her about my plan to fake a stomach ache, she knew I was anxious about sleepovers.

"I don't know. They have an alarm."

"Just ask them if they use it. Say you feel safer with the alarm on. That's all," she advised.

"Okay, I will. I'll text you if I need you. I'll try to stay!" I replied.

I casually asked Brooklyn, "So, do you guys have an alarm?"

"Yeah, my sister can't sleep without it," she said. "My parents will be home soon and they'll turn it on."

Phew! That was way easier than I expected. I always overthink things!

I changed into my pajamas, brushed my teeth, and popped a melatonin. Brooklyn's basement was like a dream! Two comfy mattresses, a cot, a cozy fireplace, and the softest carpet ever. We played games and laughed so hard our stomachs hurt. Finally, we just chatted and giggled until we were snoozing.

My dad picked me up the next morning. "We had a blast!" I told him. But then, the worry monster crept back in. *Did they like me? Did I say something dumb? What if they never wanted to hang out again?* I had to remind myself to chill out. Everything went great!

# Grandma's House

The lake was all shimmery in the sun as we pulled up to Grandma's house the next day. It was so pretty. I loved their house. It was right on the beach. And it had this old-timey feel, with a big porch swing that always creaked in the breeze. Grandma had a plate of cookies waiting for us on the kitchen table, and the whole house smelled amazing – like cookies and something warm and spicy.

Sundays were always "Grandparents Day" in our family. Every single Sunday since we moved, Grandma and Grandpa would come over for dinner. Sometimes we'd go to their house. It was awesome that we lived so close to them now. We saw them way less before.

They moved into their house when my mom was just a teenager. Even though it was on the beach, Mom never really loved it there. First of all, they didn't have city water – they had to get their water from a well! Can you imagine? So they wouldn't run out of water too fast, Grandpa only let Mom shower for three minutes! Three minutes! And Grandma could only do two loads of laundry a week. Talk about rough!

Mom said Grandma had always kept the house spotless. That was a problem now, though. Since Grandpa had his stroke, it had been harder for Grandma to keep up with cleaning and everything. I didn't really notice a difference, but Mom has this thing called OCD, which basically means she worries a lot about germs and stuff. If things aren't perfectly clean, she gets all stressed out. Since Grandma couldn't see as well anymore, the house wasn't as spotless as it used to be, and it drove Mom crazy. That was why they usually came to our house.

I loved spending time with them no matter where we were. But other things had been different since Grandpa's stroke too. He used to be so much fun! We'd play ping pong, and build crazy forts out of blankets. He'd even get down on all fours and bark like a dog! He was the best! But now he got tired so fast.

Grandma had always been fun too. She was super creative and loved to do crafts. She'd come up with the coolest stuff for us to make, even back when there was no Pinterest! She's like a real-life Pinterest board!

That Sunday though, I was feeling a little left out. It wasn't anyone's fault, but I felt like Cameron and Lizzy were getting all the attention. See, Lizzy's the baby, so she gets all the cuddles and everyone still thinks she's the cutest thing ever. The way she was talking and dancing around had everyone melting! Grandma was practically doting on her. And then there was Cameron. He and Grandpa were having this deep conversation about the universe, dinosaurs, and stuff that I didn't even understand. They talked for hours about all this crazy scientific stuff. Cameron is like a walking encyclopedia! He only reads non-fiction books because he thinks reading for fun is a waste of time. I felt like Grandpa favored him because he was so smart.

Grandpa was always super smart too. He wanted to be a doctor when he was younger, but his family couldn't afford college.

I guess I was feeling a little left out. I felt that way with my parents too. I mean, I slept over at Brooklyn's house! That was HUGE. Wasn't anyone proud of ME?

At dinner that night, I was talking about this girl in my class named Mona when Cameron just had to chime in, "Did you know that the Mona Lisa is the most famous painting in the world? It was painted by Leonardo da Vinci, and her real name isn't even Mona! It's Lisa something. And it's in the Louvre, in its own special room with bulletproof glass!"

Ugh! Did he have to know EVERYTHING? I just wanted to scream, "We know you're smart, Cameron! I'm talking now!"

I was getting a little too stressed out about this. I always overthink things. Maybe I should've tried spending the night at Grandma and Grandpa's house sometime. That might have made me feel less left out. But then, they didn't have an alarm system, and I probably would've freaked out all night.

# The Presentation

Monday morning dragged on FOREVER. My dad had to drive me to school because lugging that giant display board on the bus would have been a disaster. That meant missing the bus with Luke, which bummed me out a little.

But it felt good to be back at school with my friends. Brooklyn and Lucy were super excited to see me. I guess all my worrying about the sleepover was for nothing.

I was actually kind of excited for our presentation, even though I usually got super nervous about that stuff. I knew we were totally prepared. They were bragging about how they practiced their parts and were ready to rock the presentation.

All I could think about was seeing Luke. I kept wondering what he was wearing, if he fixed his hair… you know, the usual. As I walked out of class, I saw him leaning against my locker! My heart leaped into my throat. My cheeks probably turned beet red.

"Hi!" he said, that amazing smile of his lighting up his face.

"Hi!" I squeaked, feeling all flustered.

"You didn't tell me you weren't taking the bus this morning," he said.

"Oh yeah, totally forgot about the board," I said, trying to sound casual.

"Oh, right! That's today. You nervous?" he asked.

"Yeah, a little," I admitted.

"You'll be great! You're super smart," he said, and my cheeks burned even hotter.

"Want to walk downstairs with me?" he asked.

"Sure!" I said, feeling like I was floating.

As we walked down the stairs, he grabbed my hand! My heart was pounding so hard I thought it might jump out of my chest. I felt like everyone was staring at us. I was totally freaking out, but in a good way. He was holding my hand!

We sat down with the rest of the gang in the cafeteria. He talked to his friends, and he included me in the conversation.

I caught Nicole glaring at me from across the room. I tried to ignore her, but it was hard not to feel her icy stare.

When the bell rang, Luke offered to walk me to my locker. "Let's go," he said, and he took my hand again. Walking with him felt like it wasn't even real. I was sure everyone was watching us, but I didn't even care.

The next class was a total blur. All I could think about was Luke holding my hand. I probably didn't even pay attention to Mrs. Witt's lesson. She gave us a math assignment, and I almost forgot to even look at it.

"OMG, he held your hand!" Brooklyn squealed when I sat down. "You guys looked so cute together!"

"I know! I was freaking out," I admitted.

"He really likes you. I can tell," Brooklyn said.

"I like him a lot too," I whispered, blushing.

Presentation time. We decided to go first to get it over with.

When we walked into class, Brooklyn marched right up to Mrs. Witt. "Can we go first, Mrs. Witt? Victoria is really nervous," she said.

Mrs. Witt looked at me, and I tried to look super nervous, even though I was mostly excited. She agreed, and we set up our display board.

I started the presentation, and I was surprised at how easy it was. Having Brooklyn and Lucy there made me feel so much more confident. We worked together perfectly, and Mrs. Witt seemed really impressed.

After the presentation, I felt a huge wave of relief. We could finally relax and watch the other groups.

I took the bus home, and Luke held my hand the whole way. We didn't say much, but I didn't need to. Just being close to him made me feel happy.

When I got home, I was so excited I almost tripped over my own feet! I found my mom in her room, reading; she had only worked half a day.

"Hi Mom! How was your day?" I asked.

"Good, sweetie. How was yours?"

"Amazing!" I said. "Luke held my hand today!"

"What?! Really?" she asked, her eyes wide.

"Yep! And I think I might want to hug him sometime soon," I said, feeling a little shy.

"Victoria, you know I trust you completely. Just do what feels right," she said.

"I know, I just wanted to make sure you were okay with it."

"I'm so proud of how mature you are, sweetie," she said, pulling me into a hug.

I felt so happy and loved. It was the best feeling ever!

# Christmas Break

Christmas vacation was supposed to be the highlight of my year, but I wasn't feeling the holiday spirit. Every year, we did this epic road trip down to Florida. My grandparents had an amazing condo right on the beach, and we'd spend two weeks soaking up the sun, swimming in the pool, and eating way too much ice cream. But we weren't going to Florida this year because Grandpa hadn't been feeling well. So there'd be no Florida sun, no beach... I was going to miss it.

What I wouldn't miss was the drive to Florida. It was always a total disaster. No matter how many times Mom gave us those motion sickness pills, someone would always end up throwing up. It was seriously a family tradition. The only good part about getting there was the hotels we stayed at along the way. They always had these awesome indoor pools and huge breakfast buffets with omelet stations. I could eat pancakes and waffles until I burst!

But Christmas at home would be cool. I could finally open all my presents on Christmas morning instead of waiting until we got back from Florida. And I could hang out with Tasha! That was really the best part.

We were going to have a sleepover, go shopping, see a movie with Luke and our friends, and maybe even go sledding if it snowed. Brooklyn was off to Cancun with her family, so I wouldn't see her for a while.

I was already imagining all the fun things I was going to do. Starting with no school, no homework, just endless days of board games, movie marathons, and hot chocolate by the fireplace. Mom always goes all out with the decorations. She practically puts up the Christmas tree the day after Halloween! It's a bit much, if you ask me.

That year she went crazy with the Christmas crafts too. She bought a ton of glitter and glue and made us decorate gingerbread houses, paint ornaments, and stuff like that. I was mostly doing it to make her happy, but it was actually kind of fun.

# The Date

"It isn't what we say or think that defines us, but what we do."

– Jane Austen

Tasha had only been at my house for two hours, and it was like we were never apart. It was so easy! No matter what I did, I knew I could trust her to love me just the way I was. I still didn't feel that way with my new friends. They didn't know about my anxiety and the things I'd gone through. I wasn't convinced they would ever understand.

Tasha and I spent most of the day catching up and talking about our boyfriends. Her boyfriend, Trevor, was a guy who went to her school. We used to hang out with his twin sister, Tanya. He was super cute and really tall. It's funny that they were now dating because we always referred to him as Tanya's hot brother. Tanya used to get so grossed out by it. Tasha said that Tanya was actually happy for them. Tanya told her that Trevor had good taste. I asked her if it was weird to be friends with your boyfriend's sister. She said sometimes it was awkward, but mostly it was fine.

We were meeting a bunch of friends from my school to watch a movie. I couldn't wait! Luke was going to be there.

So far, eleven of us were going. Unfortunately, Nicole was going too. Tasha said she was just jealous that Brooklyn and I were so close. I knew where she was coming from, but I didn't get why we couldn't all be friends or why she was kept glaring at me. I was nice to her.

"I can't wait for you to meet Luke. He's so gorgeous!"

"You're so lucky your mom is letting you go, knowing he'll be there."

"She trusts me. She knows I'm not going to do anything."

"Still, my mom would never let me go on a date with Trevor; she doesn't even know I have a boyfriend."

"It's just because I tell her everything that she doesn't worry about stuff like that. Plus, we are going as a group," I explained.

I let Tasha do my makeup. She was really good at it! She watched tutorials on YouTube all the time and practiced every day after school. The only difference was that she usually did makeup on herself and her little sister, who both had dark skin, and she had never done my makeup before. But my mom bought me tons of makeup for my birthday specifically catered to gingers with light skin, so at least she would have the right palette to work with. I wanted Luke to like it.

The closer we got to leaving, the more nervous I got. I thought I was going to puke. No time for that!

"Dad, you ready to go?"

"Yep, I'm ready when you are," he yelled from the office. My dad had been spending most of his time in our home office lately. He was working on a course he'd be teaching next semester. He had to create it from scratch, and he was pretty stressed out. It was a course to prepare divers for medical emergencies. That's what he used to do. When divers are working on a ship in the middle of the ocean, they don't have doctors on board, so at least one diver has to know how to deal with stuff like the bends, and hypothermia. My dad was great in emergencies at home too. He always told us the first thing to do in an emergency is to stay calm. Try telling that to my mom. If one of us got hurt, she'd freak out like we were dying. My dad couldn't help but laugh because she did that every time, no matter how often he told her that she was making things worse. I guess she just couldn't help it. She naturally got worried about everything.

My dad dropped us off at the cinema's entrance. Through the glass doors, I could see that a lot of my friends were already there.

"Just text or call me when you want me to come get you guys," he said. As we walked in, Lily, Aliza, and Charlotte came running over to give me a group hug. It was the best greeting!

"Hi, you must be Tasha, I'm Aliza. Victoria talks about you all the time."

"Good things, right?"

"Of course!"

I noticed Nicole glaring at me from the corner of my eye, but more importantly, I saw Luke beaming. We headed over to where everyone was standing. Luke walked over and gave me a hug. I was so surprised – but thrilled. I had planned to hug him after the movie.

We all got in line to buy tickets. Standing there waiting I could smell buttery popcorn, and I hoped my stomach wouldn't turn. Then Luke bought my ticket!

"Aww, thank you, that's so sweet!" I said.

"Of course, this is our first official date. Even though I pictured it being just the two of us, I'll take it anyway."

I smiled shyly.

After getting our popcorn and snacks, we found a bunch of seats together in two rows and I squeezed in between Tasha and Luke. The movie theater was dark and cool, the only light coming from the screen. I could feel Luke's warm hand in mine, and butterflies erupted in my stomach. It felt like the whole world had stopped and it was just me and him.

After the movie, we hung out in the mall lobby for a while. I caught Nicole giving me major side-eye again, but I didn't even care. I was with my best friend, and my boyfriend. This was the best night ever!

# Tree

"A good friend will always stab you in the front."

– Oscar Wilde

The rest of Christmas break flew by faster than I though it would. I hung out with Lucy a few times after Tasha left, but honestly, I was counting down the minutes until I could see Brooklyn again. I missed her like crazy!

On our first day back, I got ready for school, feeling a mix of excitement and nerves. When I checked my phone, I saw a message from Brooklyn from the night before saying she couldn't wait to see me. I walked to the bus stop, a little nervous. But I made it without a freak out.

I was so happy to sit with Luke on the bus and walk to my locker with him. We had texted over the break, but I missed seeing him.

Then I saw THEM. A group of girls were huddled near my locker, and Brooklyn was with them looking… upset? My face lit up when I saw her. I went right over, "Brooklyn!"

She turned to face me, and instead of the smile I was expecting, she gave me the dirtiest look. Like she didn't even know me! I was totally confused. "What's wrong?" I asked, my voice trembling a little.

*What was going on? What did I miss? Was she having a bad day? Did I do something wrong? How could I?* I hadn't spoken to her since the break started, and she just texted me last night saying she couldn't wait to see me. I had to get to class so I grabbed my things and left, wondering what had just happened.

It wasn't until Lucy came into class and sat down that I could ask her what was going on. "Hey, Lucy! Why is Brooklyn ignoring me?"

"I don't know," she said vaguely. "I think she…"

We were interrupted by the national anthem and the morning announcements. I subtly looked over at Brooklyn, so she wouldn't notice. She was doing her best to avoid eye contact with me. I didn't understand what had happened. It didn't make any sense.

Once Mrs. Witt was done explaining the writing assignment, we each grabbed a Chromebook and started our work. I kept stealing glances at Brooklyn, hoping she'd look at me, but she just kept staring at her Chromebook, looking totally miserable. After I finished my plan and introduction for the assignment, I sucked it up and just came out and asked her, "Why are you mad at me?"

"Nicole told me everything on the bus this morning," she replied, her voice cold.

"Told you what exactly?"

"She told me all the mean things you said about me at the movies."

"WHAT? I didn't say anything mean about you. You know I wouldn't do that."

"Well, Lucy said she was there and that you did." I shot a look at Lucy, who was pretending to be super focused on her Chromebook.

"What the heck, Lucy!" I whispered, but she completely ignored me.

"Brooklyn, you know me; I wouldn't do that."

"Well, I don't believe you. Why would Nicole lie?"

"Maybe because she hates me and she's jealous."

"Then why would Lucy say you did?"

"I don't know! I didn't talk about you. You have to trust me." As I turned away, I felt tears filling my eyes.

I asked Mrs. Witt if I could be excused to go to the bathroom. I ran. By then, tears were streaming down my face. I locked myself in the last stall and tried not to make a sound.

*OMG, this is a disaster!* I thought, panicking. *What if Brooklyn never talks to me again? Why would Nicole do this? What did I do to deserve this?* My heart was pounding so hard I could feel it in my throat, and the room started to sway. I tried to take deep breaths, but it was impossible.

I needed to calm down. I tried to focus on my happy place: the stables back home. I tried to imagine the smell of hay, the feel of a horse's soft coat... I tried to picture myself riding through the field... I closed my eyes tighter and thought only about those things.

After what felt like forever, I had finally calmed myself down. I stood up. I couldn't hide in the bathroom all day. I had to get back to class. Looking in the mirror, I touched up my raccoon eyes and headed to the door.

Then, of all people, Nicole walked in. "Oh no, what's wrong?" she said sarcastically with a smirk on her face. "Did you lose a best friend?"

"Why would you lie like that?" I asked angrily.

"I did what I had to do. You stole her from me, and now I'm taking her back."

I was speechless. Nicole was seriously the worst.

She walked away laughing and headed into an empty stall. "Oh my gosh," I muttered to myself. "I can't believe this is actually happening."

I hid in the same bathroom stall the whole recess. Luke was probably the only one looking for me. Unless... he was mad at me too. What if Nicole got to him as well? What if everyone hated me? I quickly texted my dad, asking him to come get me. I told him I was sick. It only took him ten minutes to get to the school. He met me in the office and signed me out. He could see I wasn't good, but I wasn't ready to tell him what happened yet. I didn't think I could get it out without having a breakdown.

I spent the rest of the day crying in bed. My mom and Tasha were the only people who could help, but they were both still in school. Homework will take my mind off things, I thought. Nope. I couldn't concentrate. Luke texted me at lunch to see what happened and why I left early. I told him I didn't feel good. He was so nice and said he hoped I felt better soon. Maybe he hadn't been brainwashed by Nicole after all. There was hope!

Then horrible thoughts invaded my mind. Ruth called these dark thoughts, because I saw everything in black and forgot about all the great things I had going for me. My dark thoughts wouldn't go away. My heart hurt, my stomach hurt – everything hurt. In minutes, I had convinced myself that no one would miss me if I were gone, that everyone at school hated me, and that I was a horrible person. I kept thinking: *I am so messed up, and at least if I were gone, my parents wouldn't have to deal with me anymore. I'm just a nuisance. Everyone is better off without me.* My eyes were so filled with tears that I might as well have been blind. Those thoughts kept repeating, over and over again in my mind. I couldn't think straight. Within forty minutes, I had convinced myself that I would be better off dead!

My mom came to my room as soon as she got home.

She didn't even change her clothes. "What's wrong? Dad said you were sick." "I'm not sick," I said, sobbing. "Oh God, what happened? Did Luke break up with you?"

"No."

"Then what?"

"Tree."

That was our code word. My mom told me that when I was about a month old, she had a type of depression called postpartum depression that some women get after they have babies. She was taking medication, but she wasn't sleeping, like, at all. My dad was diving overseas then so she had been pretty much raising me on her own. One day, on her way to my grandparents' house, she started having dark thoughts. Like the kind I was having. She had trouble breathing, and all she kept thinking was that hitting a tree while going really fast would make it all go away. Her dark thoughts were taking over. She kept telling herself that no one would miss her, that she was a terrible mother, and that everyone, including me, would be better off without her. Then she started thinking about how fast she would have to drive to make sure we would die instantly and not suffer. Somehow, she managed to pull over and call my grandpa. He came to get us, and we stayed at their place until my dad came home from Dubai. So, whenever I have a dark thought, I have to find my mom and say our code word to her: tree.

"Do you have a plan?" she asked with watery eyes. "No, I just have awful thoughts," I said, sobbing. "Nicole told Brooklyn that I talked behind her back at the movies, and she believed her. Now she's mad at me and won't talk to me. Nicole somehow convinced both Brooklyn and Lucy that I did."

"How can someone be that evil? I'm so sorry! Come here." She held me so tight in her arms. I knew she would understand. I buried my face in her shoulder and just sobbed. It felt like my heart was breaking into a million pieces. "Listen, Victoria, this will all blow over. Brooklyn is not about to throw away four months of friendship just like that. Send her a text explaining everything and get her to ask anyone else who was there. Surely, someone will tell the truth." "OK, I will."

"I feel terrible for you."

"Thanks for being here, Mom."

"Anytime, honey, that's my job."

"I'm going to FaceTime Tasha if that's OK."

"Of course! Come find me when you are done, I don't want you to be alone."

Tasha was blown away. "You didn't say anything bad about Brooklyn. I should know; I was with you the whole time."

"I know, but now what do I do?"

"I have no idea."

"I can't believe Lucy. Why would she admit to something that never happened?"

"She'll do anything to fit in. Nicole is out of control! I wish I was there to give you a big hug and put her in her place."

"Me too," I sniffled.

"I feel like I'm going to explode."

I sent a text to Brooklyn explaining everything, even my confrontation with Nicole in the bathroom, but she didn't reply.

My phone buzzed with a text from Luke. It read, "Hey, are you okay? I'm worried about you." I felt a tiny bit better. Maybe not everyone hated me. There was no way I could sleep. My mom gave me six milligrams of melatonin instead of my usual three to help me relax. I watched my clock until 2:23 a.m. and eventually woke up to the sound of my alarm four hours and seven minutes later.

# Nicole

"I would rather be a little nobody, than to be an evil somebody." – Abraham Lincoln

Here's what I knew then about Nicole: She was tiny, like a pixie, with brown, wavy hair. She had an older sister. She used to take gymnastics, but then she fell off the balance beam, and it totally freaked her out. She quit after that, which was a bummer because she was really good.

Nicole wasn't great in school, but she did OK and she tried hard. Even though Brooklyn had been her best friend forever, they fought all the time! It was ridiculous. They'd argue about the silliest things – whose turn it was to pick the movie, who got to sit in the front seat of the car, even whose turn it was to go first in line at the lunchroom. They were both super competitive.

Friendships are supposed to be about trust and being there for each other, right? For Nicole, they were about having people to boss around. She wanted to be the queen bee, the most popular girl in school.

Nicole loved being the center of attention. She was always the loudest person in the room. And if someone tried to steal her spotlight, watch out! She'd find a way to bring them down. She'd start rumors, spread gossip, and even try to sabotage them. Believe me, I know.

Nicole could twist things around and make them seem like she was the victim, even when she was the one who started the trouble. She'd act all innocent and sweet to teachers and parents, but behind their backs, she was a total mean girl.

What made Nicole especially scary was that she had no problem being mean. She'd say the nastiest things, just to hurt someone else's feelings. That's what the worst bullies do. Sadly, some of the other girls, like Lucy, were just scared of her. They'd go along with whatever she wanted to do because they were afraid of getting on her bad side.

Here's what I know about Nicole now: I learned that people like Nicole are usually really insecure. I know it sounds hard to believe because they always seem so together. But it's kind of an act. Deep down, Nicole probably didn't like herself very much. And she was so afraid of other people not liking her that she tried to control them instead. She didn't feel good enough to let people like her for who she really was. Or to be ok with them not liking her.

My mom has always told me there's good in everyone. Sometimes that's hard to believe when you're dealing with someone like Nicole. All of the evil things she did were out of jealousy. She was so jealous of Brooklyn and me that she tried to sabotage our friendship.

# Hope

My stomach churned like a washing machine as I walked down the hallway. It felt like the whole school was staring, whispering, pointing. It was like I was some weird zoo animal. Nicole and her crew were probably already plotting their next move.

I tried to ignore them, but it was impossible. It was distracting me from everything else. I tried to focus on the writing assignment, but all I could hear were whispers. "Did you hear what she did?" "She's so…" I didn't even want to know the rest. My cheeks burned, and I wished I could crawl under my desk and hide.

Recess was no better. Lily, Aliza, and Charlotte were usually the life of the cafeteria, but today they were super quiet. It was like they were walking on eggshells. I went to sit with them. But I felt like a total outsider, like I didn't belong. I just wanted melt into the floorboards.

Lunch was the worst. Nicole and her gang sat a few tables away and just stared at me. I could practically hear their thoughts: *Look at her, all alone. She's such a loser.* I picked at my food, wishing I could just vanish into thin air.

Then, Nadeem. He walked by, snorting like a pig, and pointed at me. "Oink oink," he squealed, and the whole cafeteria erupted in laughter. Nicole doubled over, tears streaming down her face. It was humiliating. I wanted to cry, but I held it back, my pride stinging worse than any tears could.

But then, something good happened.

Lily.

She came over to my table, looking genuinely concerned. "Are you okay?" she asked, her voice soft.

I looked at her, surprised. "Yeah, I'm fine," I mumbled, avoiding her gaze.

"No, you're not," she said, her voice firm. "I know something's wrong."

Hesitantly, I told her about Nicole, about the rumors, about how miserable I felt. Lily listened the whole time and I could tell she cared by the look on her face.

"That's so mean," she said, shaking her head. "Nicole's just trying to make herself feel better by putting you down. Don't let her win."

Her words were like a warm hug. For the first time that day, I felt a glimmer of hope.

That weekend, I had a sleepover with Lily. We went to the ice rink for hours and had so much fun. We were honestly laughing so hard my sides ached. We stayed up late talking and I forgot all about Nicole and her mean girl games.

Lily reminded me that I wasn't alone. That I had friends who believed me and would always have my back. And that even when things felt totally hopeless, there was always a reason to smile.

# Why Me?

Monday morning felt like a punch to the gut. But I made it to school. Then I made it to class. The fluorescent lights were buzzing so loud they sounded like angry bees. It was weirdly comforting. I scanned the room, searching for Lily. But she wasn't with Aliza and Charlotte like usual. She was… with THEM.

Nicole and her minions.

My stomach lurched. *Did Nicole get to her? Did she somehow twist my words, make me look like the bad guy?* My mind raced, a whirlwind of anxieties.

"Self-talk," I muttered to myself, trying to calm down. That was something else I'd learned in therapy – talking to myself to figure out what was really going on. Usually, it helped. But today, my self-talk was just making things worse.

*Maybe I'm imagining it,* I thought. *Maybe Lily just…* But then I saw her. She was laughing with Nicole, her eyes darting nervously towards me. Guilt? Or was it just my imagination?

Recess was torture. I sat in the cafeteria alone. By then it seemed like everyone was avoiding me. It was like I was invisible.

Then, Nicole. She announced their movie plans, her voice booming across the room. "Everyone's invited… except…" she trailed off and looked over at me.

Aliza tried to include me. "You want to come, right?" she asked.

"Uh… no thanks," I mumbled, feeling a lump in my throat.

The rest of the day was a total misery. In class, I couldn't concentrate. At lunch, I ate alone. It was total isolation. And then just when I thought it was almost over, Jessica bumped into me in the hallway, spilling her juice all over me. "Oops, clumsy me," she sneered, backing away like I was covered in germs. "Gross, I touched her."

I couldn't take anymore. I ran to the bathroom, crying. Why was this happening? What had I done to deserve this?

That night, I begged my parents to let me stay home. "I can't go back there," I sobbed. "Please, anything but school!"

My mom looked heartbroken. "I know, honey, I know," she said, hugging me tight.

My dad, however, was furious. He immediately emailed the principal and told him everything. "This has gone too far," he declared, his voice trembling with anger.

It didn't matter. It wouldn't make a difference. In my mind, Nicole had already won. She had turned all my friends against me. I had no one to sit with or talk to. Not even Luke.

The next morning my body felt heavy, like I couldn't move. I had to drag myself out of bed. I was in a total fog. I was heading back upstairs after begging my dad again to let me stay home, and a chilling thought crept into my mind.

*Just jump.*

The idea was ridiculous, of course. But the thought was there, a dark whisper in the back of my mind. *It won't hurt that much,* I thought already calculating the fall. *Just a few broken bones, maybe. Then I won't have to face them.*

I leaned over the edge of the stairs and felt the railing press into my skin. The ceramic tiles below looked miles away. Cold and hard. *What if I hit my head?* So stupid. *What if I get paralyzed?*

I pulled back, my heart pounding. I sat on the step tears welling up in my eyes.

Days went by and nothing changed. School was AWFUL.

My dad was getting really frustrated. He kept emailing the principal, explaining how the girls were making my life miserable. But the principal just kept saying he'd talk to my teacher. I don't think he did because she never talked to me. All I wanted was a single day without being bullied and left out.

To try and avoid the mean girls, I started helping Mrs. Witt. Sometimes I could stay inside, but other times I had to go outside, and those girls were waiting for me when I did. I even tried hiding in the bathroom, but they found me!

"She's in there!" one of them yelled. "I can see her!"

They started laughing and making fun of me. I was crying so hard I couldn't even hear what they were saying. Then they started throwing wet toilet paper at me!

Finally, the bell rang, and I could escape. One of the girls threatened me, saying, 'Don't tell anyone about this, or we'll do something worse next time.'

When I got back to class, my teacher noticed I was upset. She asked what was wrong, and I finally told her about the mean girls.

"People will be nice to you if you're nice to them," she said.

But I knew that wasn't true. I had always been kind to everyone!

"Maybe you attract drama," she said. Like it didn't matter. Like I didn't matter! I was so shocked. I felt like she wasn't believing me or helping me at all.

The principal never talked to me about what was happening. It felt like no one was on my side.

When I got home, I told my dad everything. He was furious! He drove straight to the school.

The principal said he'd talked to the other girls, and they said I was mean to them. He reminded me they didn't have to be my friends, but he agreed they should at least be kind.

"Kind?!" my dad yelled. He was controlling his voice, but he was so mad. "They threw wet toilet paper at her!"

The principal only made excuses, saying he couldn't be everywhere at once. He even said I might be exaggerating.

The next day, he called me, Nicole, Brooklyn, and Jessica to his office. He warned us that if he had to call us in again, we'd all be suspended. I felt so alone and so scared. What were they going to do to me now?

# What's Wrong with Me?

Everything looked grey. Outside, inside, it was all the same. Luke barely looked at me in the hallway, and I didn't take the bus anymore so I couldn't sit with him. Our nightly texts had become a couple of lines before a quick "Goodnight". That's if we texted at all.

Then, one afternoon I had to take the bus because Dad couldn't pick me up. It was total tension. Luke sat by himself, just staring out the window. My heart pounded in my chest. *This is it,* I thought, a wave of dread washing over me.

He basically ignored me until I was sitting right beside him. "I… I think we should break up," he mumbled, his voice barely above a whisper.

I was crushed. I was also kind of mad. "Why?" I choked out, my voice trembling.

He looked away, avoiding me. "Nicole… they… they won't leave me alone about us. They said I had to choose between them and you." His voice trailed off.

"So, you chose them?" I whispered. If I talked any louder I knew my voice would crack.

"I… I didn't want to," he stammered, "but they… they made me feel like I had no choice."

I moved away so he wouldn't see the tears forming.

The rest of the afternoon was a blur. I walked through my house like a ghost. The dark thoughts began to creep in. They weren't leaving. *People hate me. I'm a burden. Maybe it would be better if I just… disappeared.*

That idea scared me and calmed me at the same time. I wouldn't feel lonely, or sad. I wouldn't feel anything.

I looked at the bottle of melatonin on my nightstand. Eight pills. It wouldn't hurt, would it? It would be just like falling asleep.

But then I thought of my parents. I thought of Lizzy and Cameron. Could I really do that to them? Really? I also wouldn't feel the good things anymore. This was so messed up. I was so confused.

Panic seized me. I fumbled for my phone, my fingers trembling. I dialed my mom's number. I could barely speak.

"Mom… I…" I managed to get out. I couldn't form a sentence.

"Honey, what's wrong?" she asked, her voice calm and reassuring.

"I… I need you," I choked out the word "tree" that had been trapped in my throat.

My mom stayed on the phone with me until she got home. Her face was pale and worried. She held me close in her warm arms.

"It's okay, sweetheart," she whispered, her voice soothing. "It's going to be okay."

"I was going to do it, Mom. I had a plan!" My mom held me tighter, like she was trying to hold all my broken pieces together. She didn't say a word, but I knew she understood.

"We need to go to the hospital," she whispered, her voice trembling.

"The hospital? Why?" I cried, tears were pouring down my face.

"It's not just about having dark thoughts, honey. It's about staying safe," she said, her voice firm. "We need to make sure you're okay."

The hospital was noisy and filled with worried people. I hated it. My mom held my hand so tight it almost hurt. We waited forever in the waiting room. Finally, a nurse called us into a tiny room.

"What brings you in today?" the nurse asked in a gentle voice.

My mom explained everything.

"How were you going to do it?" the nurse asked quietly.

"I was going to take a lot of melatonin," I mumbled, feeling ashamed.

She listened patiently. Her face was so understanding. "You're very brave for reaching out," she said, her voice soft. "You're not alone in this, you know."

Suddenly, my mom started crying. "My life would be empty without you," she sobbed. "You're my everything, and I can't lose you."

I hugged her as tight as I could. I couldn't say anything, but I knew how much she loved me.

Dr. Voynov, the psychiatrist, arrived shortly after. He looked young. It kind of surprised me. He asked me a bunch of questions and his voice was very calming.

"Can you tell me more about the times when you feel really worried or sad, maybe even like you don't want to keep going?" he asked in a soft voice.

Shockingly, the words tumbled out. I couldn't hold them back. I told him everything – the bullying, Luke breaking up with me, how lonely I was all the time. I felt ashamed and embarrassed.

Dr. Voynov stayed calm the whole time. He didn't interrupt me. He just listened. It felt so good to get it all out.

Then he said I needed to stay at the hospital for a while.

"I have to stay here?" I asked, immediately terrified.

"It's just for tonight," he said. His voice was still calm and it was helping. I was freaking out, but it was helping. "We want to make sure you're safe."

Safe?

I felt anything but safe. I felt trapped.

They took us to a room on the children's floor. It felt more like a cage. It was so depressing. The walls were grey, and the bed looked more like a torture device than a place to rest. There was a small camera mounted on the wall. What was that all about? I felt like I was being punished.

My mom tried to make the best of it. She unpacked a few of my favorite books, a stuffed animal, and a change of clothes. But the smell of disinfectant stuck to everything, a constant reminder of where I was.

I laid on the bed, just staring at the ceiling. The light was humming, a constant background. Mom sat beside me, her hand gently stroking my hair. "It's going to be okay, sweetheart," she whispered. I could tell she was holding back from crying. "We'll get through this."

Later, she settled into the cot beside me. I felt completely exhausted. I couldn't believe it was still the same day.

I closed my eyes still smelling the smell of disinfectant. Whatever they had given me to help me sleep worked.

When I woke up, I felt a heavy weight on my chest. Guilt. I had hurt my parents. I didn't know what to think about Lizzy and Cameron.

My mom tried to be cheerful, but I could see the worry on her face. She checked on me every few minutes, all morning long. She made sure I ate and drank. But mostly, she was just there.

Later that morning, Dr. Voynov visited. He explained that he was prescribing me some medication to help with the anxiety and depression.

"It's going to take time," he said. So calming. "But things will get better. I promise."

I wasn't sure I believed him. The world still felt grey, the joy sucked out of everything. But for the first time in weeks, I felt a flicker of hope.

# A New Day

"They were too cowardly to do what they knew to be right, as they had been too cowardly to avoid doing what they knew to be wrong."

– Charles Dickens

Weeks went by. I was feeling a little better. I started seeing a new therapist. Her name was Ms. Davis, and she was really nice. It wasn't like seeing Ruth, but still, she was helping me. The dark thoughts were under control. I knew I wasn't a burden. I knew I wasn't worthless. I knew my thoughts weren't always true.

I learned to recognize the warning signs and when to reach out for help. I also learned that I was stronger than I thought. I'm kind of proud of that.

Ms. Davis and I talked about a lot of stuff, bad and good. Because I could feel the good again! Talking about the things that worried me, made them less scary.

I changed schools and started spending more time with my new friends, doing FUN things. Not gossiping or plotting. I really liked my new school.

I realized that the "friends" I had at my old school weren't really friends at all. They were too scared to stand up for me, too afraid of becoming the next target. And I could never really trust them.

Sure, medication has probably helped me. But my family, and my real friends have helped just as much. I know they have. Medication can't heal a broken heart, only people can do that. As long as you have just one person on your side, you're never really alone.

My mom went to her high school reunion a little while ago. When she got home, she woke me up to tell me this story:

A woman named Melissa came up to her and said, "I have the coolest story to tell you!"

My mom didn't recognize her. But she loves a cool story!

Melissa said, "You probably don't remember me, but we went to the same elementary school. I was in grade four, and you were like, super cool in grade seven."

My mom said, "I'm sorry, I don't remember you."

"No worries!" Melissa said. "But listen to this! There was this kid at school who was always picking on me. He was such a jerk! Then, one day, you came up to him and said, "I see what you're doing to her. If you do it again, you'll have to deal with me!" And then you just walked away.

From that moment on, you were like a superhero to me! Whenever someone tried to mess with me, I'd say, "You see that girl with the red hair? She's my bodyguard! Mess with me, and you mess with her!"

My mom said she started crying right there. She couldn't believe she had done that! She didn't even remember it, but she knew it was something she would have done.

It just goes to show that even the smallest things can make a huge difference. My mom helped someone when they needed it most, even though she didn't know she was making such a big impact.

I wish more people had stood up for me like that when I was being bullied.

But I figured if Nicole put as much effort into being a good person as she did into being a mean girl, she might actually be a decent human being. So there's hope.

I felt sorry for her, even though she had made my life miserable. I think she wasn't happy, and that was why she was trying to bring everyone else down with her.

My experiences have taught me A LOT. I learned that bullies like Nicole need to put others down to feel better about themselves. Ms. Davis says they're like inflatable pool toys – colorful and fun, but easily punctured.

And their followers? They're not mindless robots. They're people with their own thoughts and feelings. They can choose to be a follower, or stand up for what's right. Sadly, it's easier to just go along with the crowd.

I also learned that true strength means standing up for what you believe in, even when it's hard. That true friends are the ones who have your back, no matter what.

Of course, I'm still learning and growing. But I'm braver now, and I really get how other people might be hurting too. I notice when they're struggling because I've been there. And I'll do my best to help them. I know I can handle whatever tough stuff comes my way. Even when people try to bring me down, I can still find something good.

And most importantly, I know that I am not alone.

"I have been bent and broken but – I hope – into a better shape."

– Charles Dickens